Shimmer & Shine

A Tale of Two Genies

SHIMMER AND SHINE: A TALE OF TWO GENIES

A CENTUM BOOK 978-1-910917-25-1

Published in Great Britain by Centum Books Ltd

Centum Books Ltd, 20 Devon Square, Newton Abbot, Devon, TQ12 2HR, UK.

books@centumbooksltd.co.uk

CENTUM BOOKS Limited Reg. No. 07641486

This edition published 2016

A CIP catalogue record for this book is available from the British Library.

Printed in China

1 3 5 7 9 10 8 6 4 2

Based on the TV series Shimmer and Shine™

nickelodeon

A Tale of Two Genies

Adapted by David Lewman
from the script "My Secret Genies" by Sindy Boveda Spackman
Illustrated by Dave Aikins

It was a beautiful morning in Zahramay Falls. Shine jumped out of bed.

"Nahal, my sweet little tiger, I am so excited!" she smiled. "Today is the day my twin sister, Shimmer, and I become genies! We finally get to grant wishes for our new friend. Let's go wake up Shimmer."

But Shimmer wasn't in her bedroom. Shine searched and searched but couldn't find her twin sister anywhere.

"Where in the genie world did she go?" Shine asked.

Shine and Nahal looked all over the palace. They spotted a collection of pretty genie bottles. Suddenly, one began to shake and out popped Shimmer and her pet monkey, Tala!

"What's with all the bottles, sis?" Shine asked.

"I'm looking for one to give to our new friend," Shimmer explained.

Shine laughed. “We can’t use any old genie bottle. We have to make a new one.”

Shimmer clapped her hands and the genies’ magic carpet appeared. “Come on, let’s go find some special ingredients to make it with.”

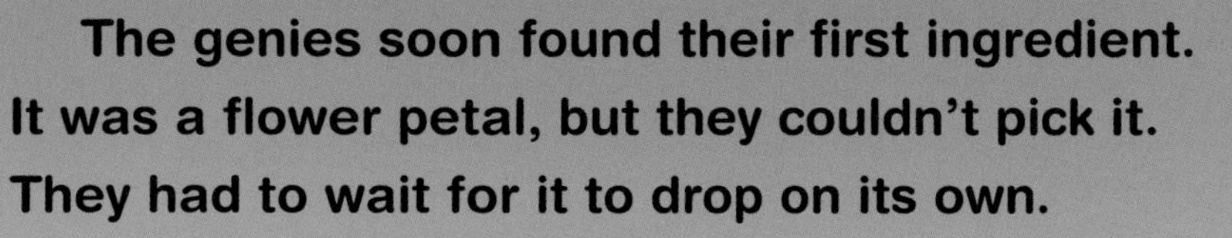

The genies soon found their first ingredient. It was a flower petal, but they couldn't pick it. They had to wait for it to drop on its own.

"As genies-in-training," explained Shimmer, "we might make mistakes, so we will need a friend with a lot of patience!"

Finally a petal fell from the flower and Shine placed it in a glittering box.

Shimmer clapped her hands for their magic carpet and they flew off to find the next ingredient.

"Let's make some fun sand castles," Shine suggested as they flew over a sandy beach.

"Good idea!" Shimmer agreed. "Our new friend should be fun too."

Shimmer magically added a whole sand castle into a jar. They had their second ingredient.

The genies hopped on their magic carpet and flew high into the sky and through a cloud.

"Whoa!" exclaimed Shine. "That cloud looks like a heart!"

"It does," Shimmer agreed, grabbing some of the cloud. "We need a puff of this cloud to match our friend's kind heart!"

Shimmer and Shine swooped down towards the ocean. They used their magic carpet like a surfboard to ride the waves.

"Surfing takes a lot of bravery," Shine said. "And our new friend has to be brave, too."

Shimmer collected a drop of the wave for their next ingredient.

The genies soared through the magical Garden of Hanging Stars. “We need to find a really special star,” Shine said. “Something unique, like our friend should be.”

Tala pointed to a large sparkling star.

"Yes, that's the one!" Shimmer thanked Tala.

"Now that we've got all the ingredients, let's go mix them together!" Shine smiled.

Back at the palace, Shine put the ingredients into a bowl and clapped her hands. A beautiful bottle appeared.

Next, the genies shrank the bottle so it was the right size to fit a necklace charm. It was perfect! But who would they give it to?

The twins ran to ask the Magic Mirror. The mirror spun around and around until it showed the perfect friend for them. Someone patient, fun, kind-hearted, brave and unique.

The genies sent the genie bottle into the human world. It attached itself to a necklace on a fairground stall.

At the fairground, a girl named Leah knocked over some milk bottles with a ball.

"Well done. You have won a prize," the stall owner told her. "Which prize would you like?"

Leah looked at the prizes and wanted the necklace. But her best friend, Zac, said, "Oooh! Get the walkie-talkies!" Giggling, Leah agreed.

The stall owner was impressed that Leah had chosen a prize for her friend. He let her pick out another prize. Leah chose the pretty necklace.

"You know, I don't think I've ever seen this prize here before," the stall owner told her. "Maybe it's magical and there are genies inside."

Leah didn't believe in genies but when the bottle on her new necklace began to glow, she was curious and gave it a rub. Colorful smoke and sparkles swirled out of it.

"What's happening?" she exclaimed.

Poof! Leah couldn't believe her eyes! Two girls, a little monkey and a baby tiger magically appeared. Shimmer and Shine gave Leah a huge hug.

"Who are you?" asked Leah, confused.

"I'm Shimmer!" smiled the girl with the pink ponytail.
"I'm Shine!" said the one with big lavender eyes.
Together they chimed, "Your genies divine!"
"We're here to grant you three wishes a day." Shine explained.
"There's no way you're real genies," Leah said.
"Oh yes we are," Shimmer said. "We'll show you!"

Using their genie magic, Shimmer and Shine made skateboards, sundaes and a tree house appear.

"WOW!" Leah was amazed. "You truly are genies."

The sisters jumped up and high-fived. "Zahara zlam!"

"That means 'awesome' in Genie," Shine explained.

Leah hugged the genies. "I'm so lucky to have my very own genies!"

Shimmer smiled. "You're patient, fun, kind-hearted, brave and unique."

Shine added, "So *we're* the lucky ones to have *you*!"

Read it Again Activities

Can you answer the questions below now you have read the story? If you're not sure of the answers, then read the story again.

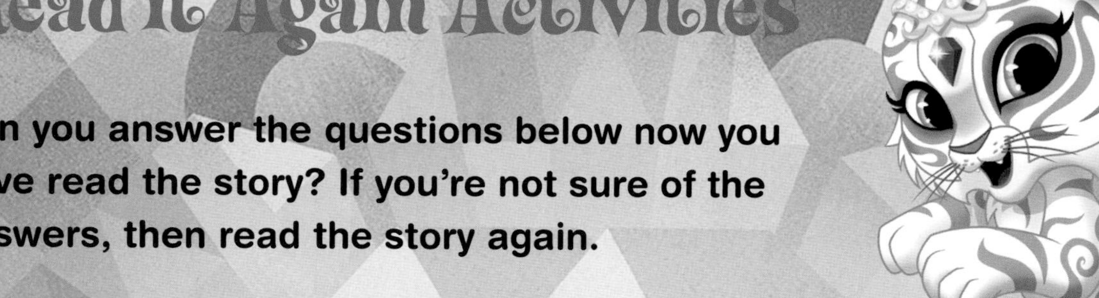

1. Why was Shine excited when she woke up?
2. What colour was the petal the genies used as their first ingredient?
3. What shape was the cloud that the sisters flew through?
4. What did Shimmer and Shine use to surf on the ocean waves?
5. Where did Leah win her necklace charm prize?

Check your answers on page 32.

Lots to Spot

Read the story again. Can you find the things below in the pages?

Nahal

Star

Sand Castle

Blue Flower

Tala

Skateboard

Check your answers on page 32.

Spot the Difference

Can you spot **6** differences between these **2** pictures of Shimmer and Shine?

Check your answers on page 32.

Magical Charm

Make your own special magical charm like the one Shimmer and Shine give to Leah. Don't forget to ask a grown-up to help you.

What you need

- a small clean jar or bottle
- paint and paintbrush
- water
- glitter
- special ingredients

SHIMMER'S TIP!

Why not make a few magical charms to give to your friends, so they can make their wishes come true, too.

What to do

- Paint a pretty pattern on your jar or bottle and leave to dry.
- Add some water and glitter to the jar or bottle.
- Choose three special ingredients to go into your jar or bottle. These could be a flower petal, a small pebble or a leaf.
- Put the lid on your jar or bottle and give it a shake to mix up the magic.
- Close your eyes, give the jar or bottle a rub and make a wish.

Magic Carpet Picnic

Have your own magic carpet adventure and plan the perfect picnic for you and your friends. Don't forget to ask a grown-up's permission and for their help in organising.

What you need

- a rug, sheet or picnic blanket for your magic carpet
- some delicious snacks to eat
- water, milk or juice to drink

Who to invite

Invite your friends, your family or even your toys to join you on your magic carpet adventure.

Where?

Find a quiet spot in your house, where you can spread out your carpet and have lots of space to play. If it's a sunny day, why not have your picnic outdoors in your garden or a park.

SHINE'S TIP!

Don't forget your carpet is a magic one, so close your eyes, make a wish and your picnic can be anywhere you want it to be!

Answers

Read It Again Activities

1 Shine was excited because today was the day she and her sister Shimmer were going to become genies.

2 The flower's petals were blue.

3 The cloud was a heart shape.

4 Shimmer and Shine surfed the ocean waves on their magic carpet.

5 Leah won her charm necklace prize at the fairground.

Lots To Spot

Nahal – page 6

Star – page 15

Sand castle – page 11

Blue flower – page 9

Tala – page 7

Skateboard – page 25

Spot The Difference